Phonics Focus: long a (ai)

Your
BRAIN

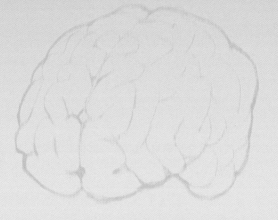

BY CHRISTINA EARLEY

**ILLUSTRATED BY
ANASTASIA KLECKNER**

A Blue Marlin Book

SEAHORSE
PUBLISHING

Introduction:

Phonics is the relationship between letters and sounds. It is the foundation for reading words, or decoding. A phonogram is a letter or group of letters that represents a sound. Students who practice phonics and sight words become fluent word readers. Having word fluency allows students to build their comprehension skills and become skilled and confident readers.

Activities:

BEFORE READING

Use your finger to underline the key phonogram in each word in the *Words to Read* list on page 3. Then, read the word. For longer words, look for ways to break the word into smaller parts (double letters, word I know, ending, etc.).

DURING READING

Use sticky notes to annotate for understanding. Write questions, make connections, summarize each page after it is read, or draw an emoji that describes how you felt about different parts.

AFTER READING

Share and discuss your sticky notes with an adult or peer who also read the story.

Words to Read:

air	afraid	mermaid
bait	aided	obtain
pair	attain	painting
rains	await	rainbow
raised	daily	refrain
tails	dairy	repair
brain	daisy	sailboat
chain	details	sailfish
quail	email	acquainted
snail	explain	
train	fairy	

The brain is a special part of your body.

It is used daily to do many different things.

6

Your brain helps you write an email.

You can explain how you used bait to obtain a sailfish on a fishing trip.

Were you afraid it would pop off the line as you raised it in the air?

When it rains and the sun is shining, your brain tells you to look for a rainbow.

Use your brain to look at the details in the picture. Do you see a fairy sitting in a daisy? Is the mermaid to the left or right of the sailboat?

Does the chain on the train need a repair? Is there a painting of a snail or a quail? Can you find the pair of dairy cows with black tails?

Your brain aided you with this task.

Refrain from being afraid. Get acquainted with your brain.

Work hard to attain the dreams that await you!

Quiz:

1. **True or false?** The brain is an important part of the body.

2. **True or false?** Your brain helps you look closely at details.

3. **True or false?** The brain is needed to write stories.

4. How does your brain know when to look for a rainbow?

5. What is the genre of this book? How do you know?

Flip the book around for answers!

Answers:
1. True
2. True
3. True
4. It knows that a rainbow is created when light shines through water.
5. Nonfiction, because it gives facts and explains real things.

Activities:

1. Write a story about how you use your brain to do an activity.

2. Write a new story using some or all of the "ai" words from this book.

3. Create a vocabulary word map for a word that was new to you. Write the word in the middle of a paper. Surround it with a definition, illustration, sentence, and other words related to the vocabulary word.

4. Make a song to help others learn the long a sound of "ai."

5. Design a game to practice reading and spelling words with "ai."

Written by: Christina Earley
Illustrated by: Anastasia Kleckner
Design by: Rhea Magaro-Wallace
Editor: Kim Thompson
Educational Consultant: Marie Lemke, M.Ed.
Series Development: James Earley

Library of Congress PCN Data
Your Brain (ai) / Christina Earley
Blue Marlin Readers
ISBN 978-1-6389-7999-9 (hard cover)
ISBN 979-8-8873-5058-5 (paperback)
ISBN 979-8-8873-5117-9 (EPUB)
ISBN 979-8-8873-5176-6 (eBook)
Library of Congress Control Number: 2022944999

Printed in the United States of America.

Seahorse Publishing Company

seahorsepub.com

Published in the United States
Seahorse Publishing
PO Box 771325
Coral Springs, FL 33077